THREE POCKETS FULL

A story of love, family, and tradition.

Written by Cindy L. Rodriguez

Illustrated by Begoña Fernández Corbalán

THREE POCKETS FULL

A story of love, family, and tradition

Summary: Beto accepts that Mami is getting remarried after avoiding the subject and attempting to rid himself of the guayabera, a traditional Mexican wedding shirt.

Our books may be purchased in bulk for promotional, educational or business use. Please contact your local bookseller or Baker & Taylor Publisher Services: www.btpubservices.com

LCCN: 2021942967
ISBN (hardcover): 978-1-7353451-5-4
ISBN (Ebook): 978-1-7353451-6-1

The art in this book was created using Adobe® Photoshop® software.

Book design by Maggie Spurgeon

CARDINAL RULE PRESS
5449 Sylvia
Dearborn Heights, MI 48125

www.CardinalRulePress.com

Before Reading

- Read the title and look at the cover. Ask your child to predict what the story will be about.
- Tell your child a guayabera is a shirt often worn in Latin American countries and is also called a Mexican traditional wedding shirt.
- The guayabera has four pockets. If your child had a guayabera, what would they put in the pockets? Why?
- The subtitle mentions traditions. Talk about traditions celebrated in your family.
- Has your child ever had to do or wear something that they didn't want to? When? How did they feel? What was the outcome?

While Reading

- Beto says he doesn't want to go to the wedding or wear the guayabera. He doesn't say why. Before the end of the story, talk about Beto's resistance both to the wedding and the shirt. Why did he feel this way?
- How does Beto try to rid himself of the guayabera? How would you try to get rid of it?
- How do you think Beto feels each time the guayabera ends up back in his bedroom?

After Reading

- Ask your child to retell the story in their own words.
- Talk to your child about avoidance, facing fears or having hard conversations, and acceptance, and the emotions that go along with these, using Beto as an example.
- Beto leaves one of his pockets empty. Why? What do you think he might fill it with eventually?
- By the end of the book, how do we know Beto has accepted that Mami is getting remarried and that the shirt is a part of their cultural and family traditions?

For my dad,
who looks super cool
in a guayabera.

C.L.R.

To my family
who is always my
inspiration.

B.F.C.

I'm **not** wearing a guayabera to the wedding!

NOPE! NUNCA!
Not going to happen!

I don't even want to go to the wedding.

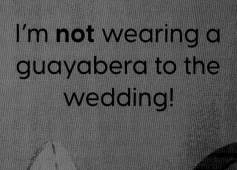

I COUGH.

I SNEEZE.

I WHEEZE.

"You're perfectly healthy," Mami says after a quick check of my eyes, ears, nose, and throat.

When Mami isn't looking,
I low-crawl into her room and
chuck the shirt onto her bed.

A note shoved in one of the pockets says:

Thanks, but no gracias. I have way cooler shirts.

Later that day, the shirt is back on my bed with Mami's note:

This is 100% cotton. Perfect for a hot day! You'll be super cool wearing it.

NOPE! NUNCA!

Not going to happen!

The next day, I slide Lupe's front legs into the shirt sleeves, then lob her ball into the living room.

I was panting, so Beto loaned me this shirt. It is super cool! I think I'll keep it.

If Beto has to go to the wedding, he wants to wear something traditional, like a tuxedo.

love,

Later, Lupe leaps onto my bed with a new note peeking out of her pocket.

The guayabera is a traditional shirt in Latino communities. You know this. It's also called the Mexican wedding shirt, so it's perfect for the occasion!

Of course you must go.

Please take it off Lupe. She hates wearing clothes.

The next day, I attack from the skies.

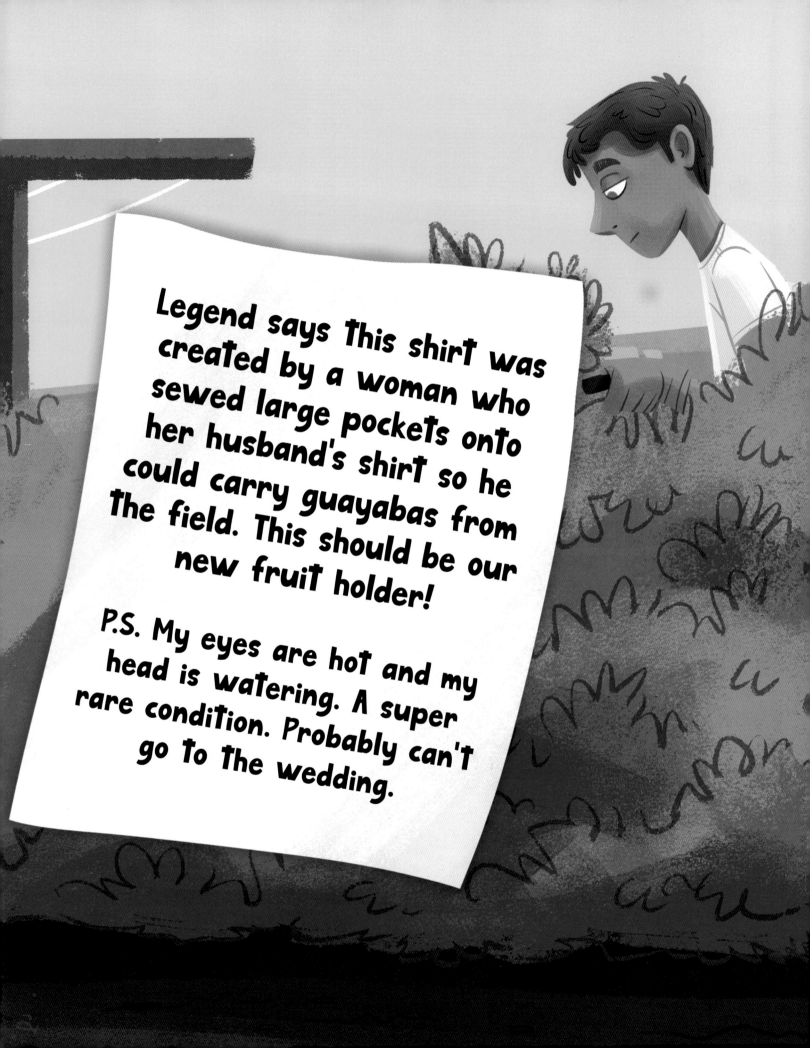

Later, the shirt is back on my bed – no note.
Great. Now we're not talking at all.

I guess this is Mami's
way of saying,

"Enough, Beto. Basta ya."

But it isn't enough.

I'm **not** wearing
this shirt.

And I'm **not** going
to the wedding!

NOPE!
NUNCA!

NOT going to happen!

I sneak into the basement and search for a place to hide the shirt.

When I remove a box top, Papi's smile greets me.

I flip through a stack of pictures I haven't seen before — pictures of Papi, and Abuelo, and even Bisabuelo.

And Mami looks happy.

For a long time she wasn't happy, but now she is again.

"I miss him,"

I say to Mami,
who has found me.

**"I miss him, too, Beto.
I always will,"**

says Mami.

Mami's wedding
day is here.

I wear my super
cool guayabera.

Mami's ring in
one pocket,
David's ring
in another,

the picture of
Papi, Abuelo, and
Bisabuelo in the third,
and that last one is
empty, waiting to be
filled.

Author's Note:

The origin of the guayabera is uncertain. The popular legend is that 300 years ago, a Spanish settler in Cuba asked his wife to sew four large pockets to the front of his shirt so that he could easily pick and carry guayabas (guavas). Its origin, however, has been debated and no one is really sure if it came from Cuba, Mexico, Thailand, or the Philippines.

The guayabera is a functional, traditional shirt that is made with materials to keep a person cool in hot weather. The most traditional guayaberas are white or light in color, have two or four pockets on the shirt front, two vertical rows of small pleats and/or embroidery, a straight hem, and is meant to be worn untucked.

The shirt can be worn for casual, business, or formal occasions, including weddings and political events. It is known as a Mexican wedding shirt and is Cuba's "official dress garment" for men.

In Mexico, March 21 has been declared Día de la Guayabera, on the same day as the beginning of spring, the season of the year which is ideal for a change of wardrobe.

Cindy L. Rodriguez is the author of the YA novel *When Reason Breaks* and has contributed to the anthology *Life Inside My Mind: 31 Authors Share Their Personal Struggles*. She has also written the text for three *Jake Maddox* books: *Volleyball Ace, Drill Team Determination,* and *Gymnastics Payback*.

Before becoming a teacher in 2000, she was an award-winning reporter for The Hartford Courant and researcher for The Boston Globe's Spotlight Team. She is a founder of Latinxs in Kid Lit, a blog that celebrates children's literature by/for/about Latinxs. Cindy is currently a middle school reading specialist in Connecticut, where she lives with her family.

This is her debut picture book.

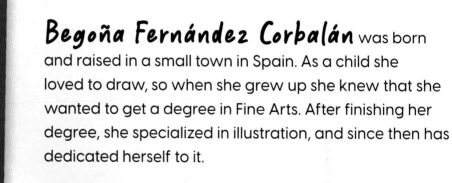

Begoña Fernández Corbalán was born and raised in a small town in Spain. As a child she loved to draw, so when she grew up she knew that she wanted to get a degree in Fine Arts. After finishing her degree, she specialized in illustration, and since then has dedicated herself to it.

In her free time she likes to sit in the sun in the garden and observe how the light changes at different times of the day, something that she tries to reflect in her work. She has worked with techniques such as watercolor, gouache and colored pencil, but she sticks to digital illustration because of the great advantages it offers when working.

October Smiled Back

Written by LISA WESTBERG PETERS

Illustrated by ED YOUNG

Henry Holt and Company · New York

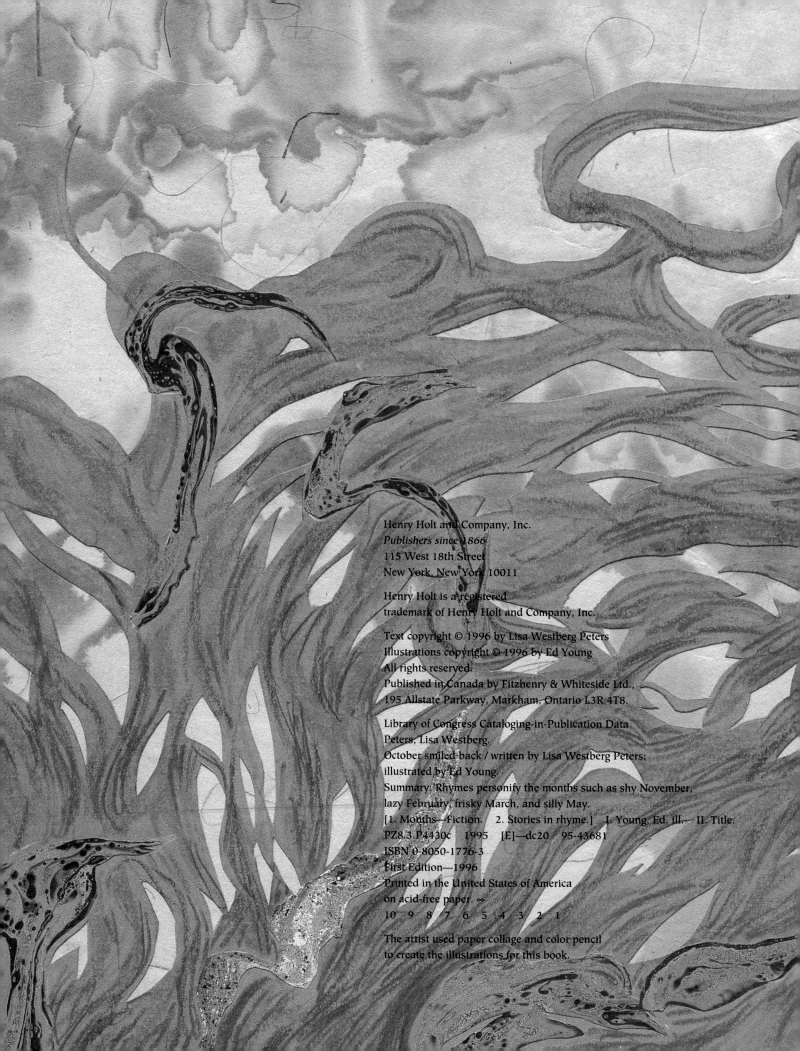

Henry Holt and Company, Inc.
Publishers since 1866
115 West 18th Street
New York, New York 10011

Henry Holt is a registered
trademark of Henry Holt and Company, Inc.

Published in Canada by Fitzhenry & Whiteside Ltd.,
195 Allstate Parkway, Markham, Ontario L3R 4T8.

Library of Congress Cataloging-in-Publication Data
Peters, Lisa Westberg.
October smiled back / written by Lisa Westberg Peters;
illustrated by Ed Young.
Summary: Rhymes personify the months such as shy November,
lazy February, frisky March, and silly May.
[1. Months—Fiction.   2. Stories in rhyme.]   I. Young, Ed, ill.— II. Title.
PZ8.3.P4430c   1995   [E]—dc20   95-43681
ISBN 0-8050-1776-3
First Edition—1996
Printed in the United States of America
on acid-free paper. ∞
10 9 8 7 6 5 4 3 2 1

The artist used paper collage and color pencil
to create the illustrations for this book.

To all my October friends

—L. W. P.

To Joanna King, for her enthusiasm, vision, and inspiration to the child within all of us

—E. Y.

Shy November looked out with her eyes puddle-gray.
I peeked in and whispered, "Come on . . .

. . . want to play?"

So December and I made a woolly white bear
Who could wink with one eye and had icicle hair.

But when January froze all her fingers and toes.
We played jungle inside in our tropical clothes.

Lazy February yawned. She was grumpy and bored.

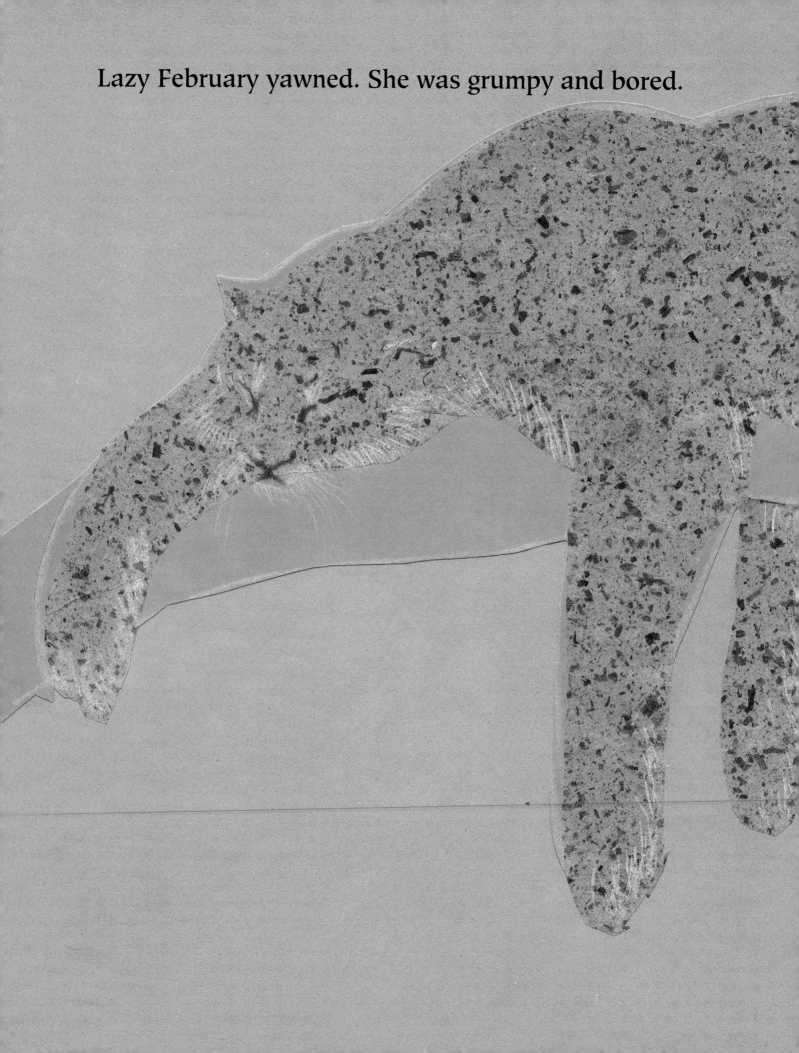

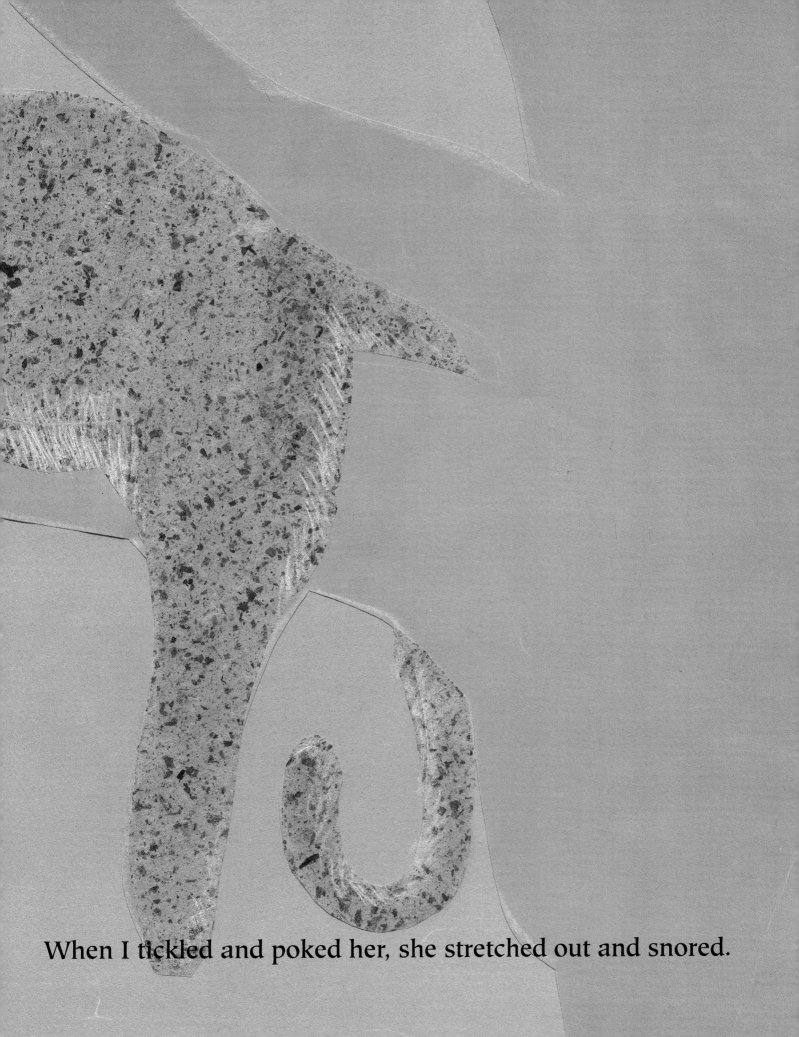

When I tickled and poked her, she stretched out and snored.

Frisky March tossed her head and shook off her sleep.
She had spring in her laugh and spring in her leap.

In a rush, April galloped right past me to find
Bigger pastures to run in. I stayed behind.

Silly May picked new friends as if they were flowers.
I hid in my cave playing dragon for hours.

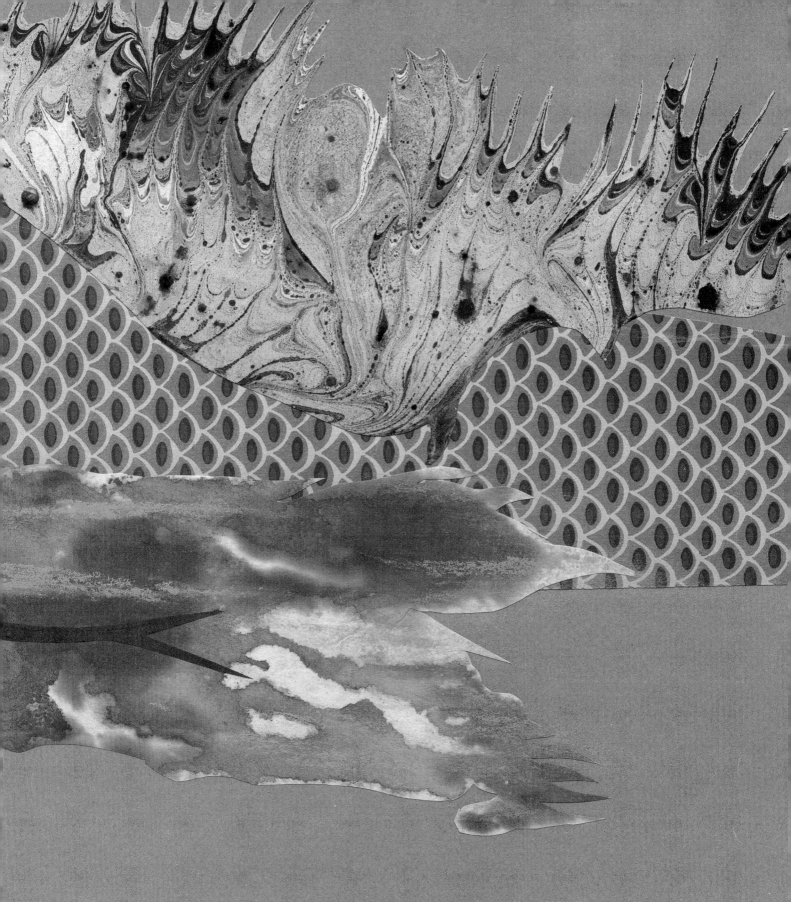

When June looked for me, I was busy with things
Like breathing blue fire and trying my wings.

July and I hardly remembered our fun
As it faded away in the glare of the sun.

August said she'd return, but she didn't say when.

I wondered if I'd ever see her again.

"There she is!" My words floated like leaves on the breeze.
"September," I whispered, "let's play again, please?"

When October smiled back, I knew I would spend
Half the night throwing stars with a friend . . .

. . . an old friend.